Storybook Treasury

© 1997 Disney Enterprises, Inc.
Printed in the United States of America
1 3 5 7 9 10 8 6 4 2

Table of Contents

A Whale of a Tale

One beautiful summer afternoon, a family of whales were swimming and playing near the surface of the sea. Suddenly they heard sailors calling from a whaling ship.

"Whales! Whales! After them!" the sailors shouted.

As the ship raced toward them, the whales swiftly swam away. Soon they had escaped the ship. But in the confusion, one little whale was left behind. Alone and frightened, it swam in circles crying for its mother.

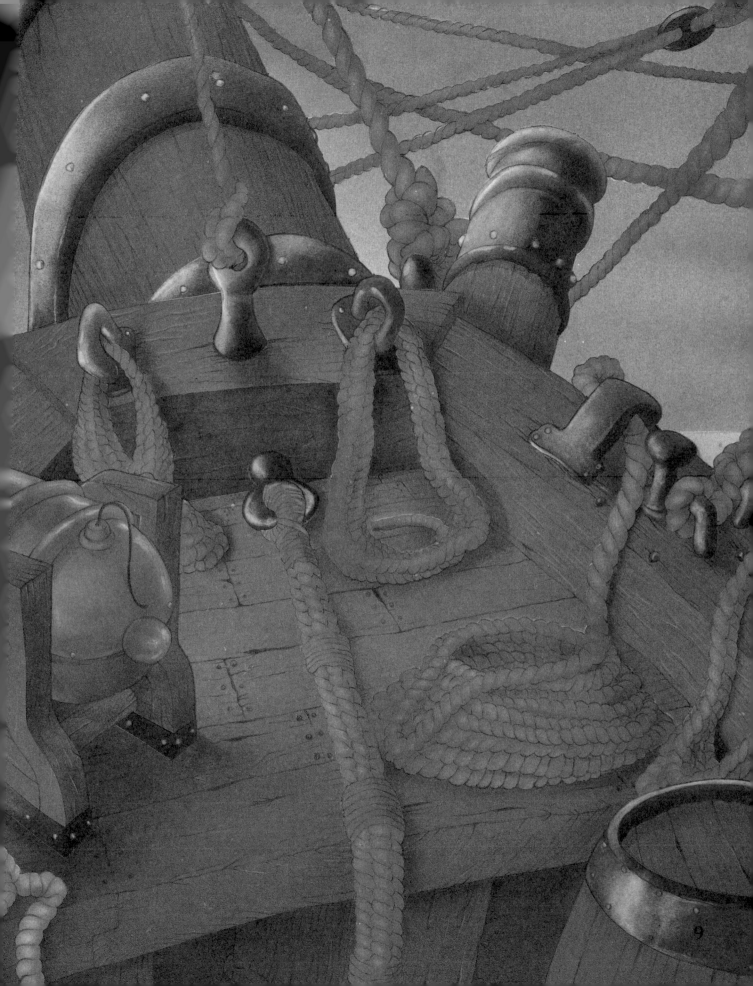

Ariel and Flounder were playing nearby when they heard the little whale's cries. "Listen, Flounder, I think someone is calling for help," Ariel said. "We'd better go see."

"It sounds to me like someone is calling for lunch," Flounder gulped. But Ariel was already swimming toward the sound.

"Ariel, wait!" Flounder called, racing after her. As he zipped around a rock, he came face to face with the little whale!

"Aaaah! A whale! A killer whale!" Flounder shrieked.

Just then, Ariel appeared. "Oh, isn't he an adorable little fellow," she said.

"Little? Adorable?" Flounder gulped. "His teeth are bigger than I am!"

The little whale snuggled close to Ariel and whimpered.

"Oh, Flounder, he's lost and sad," Ariel said, stroking the whale's nose. "I'm going to name him Spot and take him home with me. You can be his big brother! We'll be his family."

"Well," Flounder said thoughtfully, "that does sound nice."

As Ariel and Flounder started to lead the little whale home, they saw Sebastian heading their way.

"Uh-oh," Ariel said. "Hurry, Flounder. We have to hide Spot. If Sebastian sees him, he'll really be angry." Quickly, Ariel sneaked Spot into her room and hid him beneath her bedcovers.

17

"Ariel, where have you been?" Sebastian asked, entering Ariel's room. "I've been looking for you everywhere. It's time to practice for the big Spring Celebration."

Just then, Spot made a funny noise. "What's that sound?" Sebastian asked, pulling back the covers. "What is this whale doing here?" he yelled when he saw Spot.

"He followed me home," Ariel explained. "I'm going to keep him."

"And I'm going to be his big brother," Flounder chimed in.

"Are you both crazy?" Sebastian shouted. "Whales aren't house pets! I'm going to tell the King."

"Oh, please, Sebastian, Spot won't survive on his own," Ariel cried. "Please don't tell."

"Okay, I won't tell," Sebastian agreed with a sigh. "But if your father finds out about this, I'm crab cakes for sure."

"Thank you! " Ariel exclaimed, hugging Sebastian. As Spot leapt happily, his huge tail smacked Sebastian across the room.

Soon it was time for the Spring Celebration. "Stay here, Spot. I'll be back soon," Ariel told the little whale as she and Flounder left for the concert.

When they arrived, Sebastian was onstage singing.

King Triton listened politely to Sebastian's song.
Spot left Ariel's room to peek in on the concert. It was lucky
for Spot that nobody noticed him watching the performance.

A snappy chorus sang along with Sebastian. Soon the whole audience was singing and clapping along. What a show! It was one of Sebastian's best concerts.

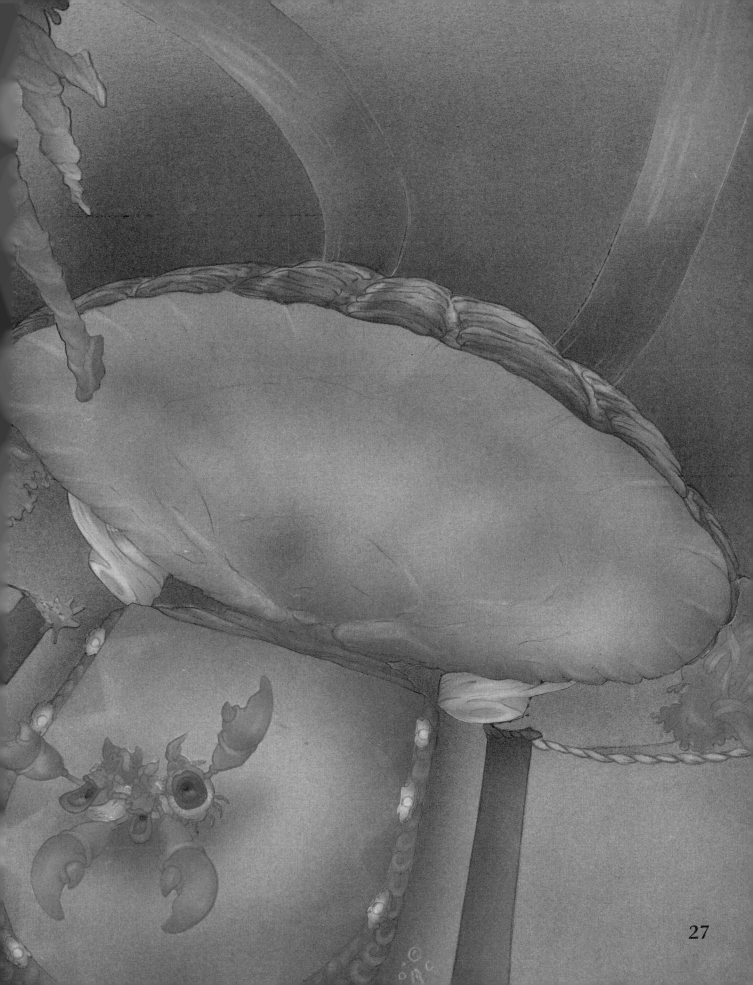

Spot listened to the music. It was so bright and lively, he began to sing along. Then he swam right into the concert hall.

Suddenly, to Sebastian's surprise, Spot was on the stage singing right along at the top of his voice.

Then Spot began to dance to the music, too. Back and forth his huge tail went, keeping time with the beat. Faster and faster went the music. Faster and faster went Spot's enormous tail.

CRASH! Spot's tail hit a column, knocking it over. THUNK! He accidentally smashed another column. As the concert hall began to crumble, everyone ran out. The concert was over.

30

King Triton was furious. "The whole palace could have been destroyed by that whale," he shouted at Ariel.

"Spot didn't mean any harm," Ariel protested. "He just loved the music so much, he got too excited."

"I understand," Triton replied, more gently. "But a palace is no place for a whale! He doesn't belong here. He'll have to leave."

"But Daddy, Spot doesn't know how real whales live," Ariel pleaded. "He can't survive on his own."

"Then you and Flounder and Sebastian will have to teach him how," Triton replied. "And I'm giving you just two weeks."

"Oh boy," Sebastian groaned. "We're in over our heads now, that's for sure."

The next day, Ariel, Sebastian, and Flounder began Spot's lessons. "Spot, you must learn to protect yourself against sharks," Sebastian explained. "So Flounder's going to pretend to be a shark. When you see him coming, bump him with your head and bang him with your tail."

Flounder made a fierce face. "Here comes the terror of the deep, Flounder the Tiger Shark," he shouted, swimming straight at Spot.

Poor little Spot took one look at Flounder and was terrified!
With a fearful cry, he started racing toward the palace.

"Spot, Spot, come back!" Ariel cried, swimming after him.
Flounder and Sebastian hurried close behind.

"Wow! I must have been really scary," Flounder said just a
bit proudly.

"I just don't think Spot understands," Ariel answered sadly.
"Oh dear, how are we going to help him learn?"

It was almost bedtime when they reached home. "Poor Spot,
you look so tired," Ariel said. "I'll put you to bed." But Sebastian
shook his head.

"Spot can't sleep in your room anymore," he told Ariel.
"Whales sleep outdoors. How are you going to teach him
to live in the sea, if you treat him like a baby?"

41

"You're right, Sebastian," Ariel agreed sadly. "But if Spot has to stay outside, then I'm staying with him!"

"Me, too!" Flounder piped up.

"I think you're both crazy," Sebastian fussed. "But somebody has to keep an eye on you. I guess I'll stay outside with you, too."

Ariel, Flounder, and Sebastian snuggled up in Spot's fins. Soon they were all asleep.

In the morning, the threesome took Spot out for another lesson. "Come on, let's try that shark fighting part again," Sebastian said. But Spot just wanted to play.

Suddenly, without warning, three ferocious sharks attacked the little group!

"Swim, Flounder!" Ariel yelled. "Swim, Spot!"

But the sharks came closer every second.

"Head for cover!" Sebastian shouted, leading his friends into a large shell. But the sharks just ripped the shell open with their sharp teeth.

Ariel, Flounder, and Sebastian were surrounded. "Help! Help!" Flounder yelled as the sharks snapped their huge jaws and lunged at them.

Suddenly, Spot knew what to do. POW! He banged the sharks with his head. THUMP! He smacked them with his tail. Quickly, the sharks fled.

"Spot, you saved our lives," Ariel, Flounder, and Sebastian shouted. As they cheered, a pod of whales swam by. Spot gave a happy cry of recognition.

Ariel and her friends hugged Spot goodbye. "Go be with your family," Ariel said. "But remember, we'll always be your friends."

Then, with a happy farewell flip of his tail, the little whale went home where he belonged.

Charmed

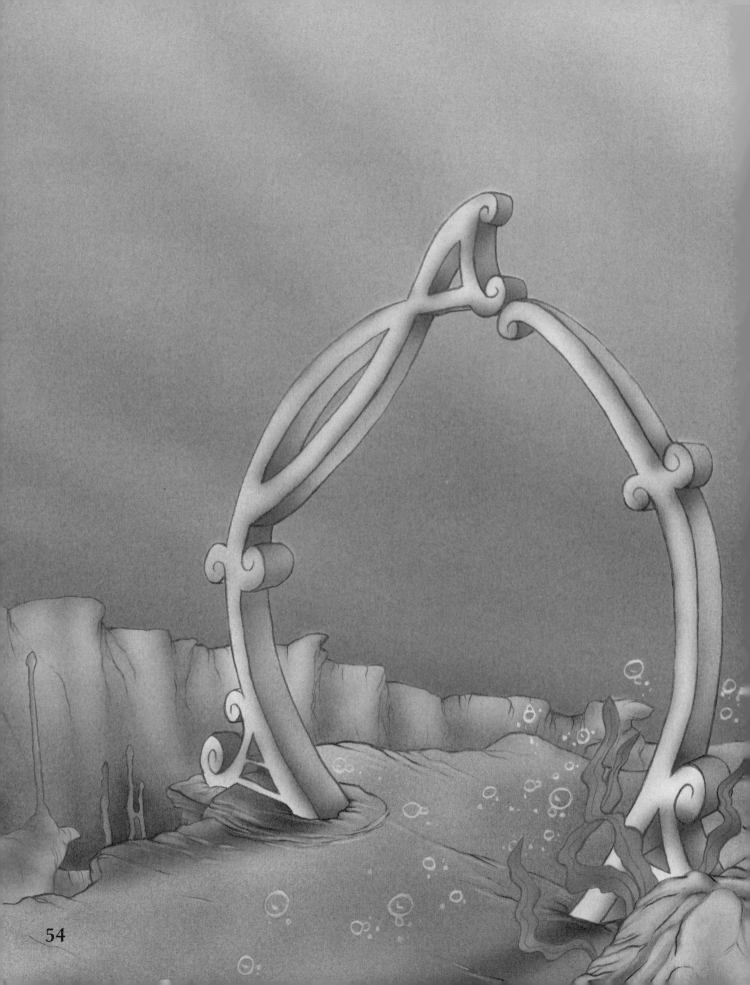

Ariel, the Little Mermaid, was lonely. Her friend Flounder had been swimming around with some fish from his school all day; Sebastian had been working on composing a new song; and her father…well, he was always busy.

In fact, he had been so busy recently that he had practically spent no time at all with the Little Mermaid. Suddenly Ariel had an idea…

When Ariel arrived at the palace, her father was in the midst of judging an octopus arm-wrestling match.

"Ariel!" cried King Triton. "What a pleasant surprise!"

"I just wanted to see if you could go for a swim," replied the Little Mermaid.

King Triton did want to spend some time with her, but being a king was no easy task.

"I'm sorry," King Triton replied. "I have to finish my work here. Maybe we can go out later."

"That's all right," Ariel sighed as she swam away. "I was just hoping we could spend some time together."

Outside the palace, Ariel decided to go exploring, so she headed toward an old sunken ship. Suddenly she heard a little gurgle behind her. When she turned to see what it was, there was Flounder!

"Boo!" said Flounder with a giggle. "Did I scare you, huh? Did I?"

Ariel wasn't scared, but she sure was glad to see her good friend again. "Come with me to explore that sunken ship," she said. "I'll bet it's filled with lots of human things!"

Sure enough, Ariel and Flounder soon found themselves discovering lots of interesting things inside the sunken ship. Flounder found a funny moving picture that made faces back at him.

Ariel found a round piece of glass on a stick.

"Flounder, look what I found," she cried. "When I look through it, it makes everything look big!"

"Wow!" said Flounder. "What do you call that thingamajigger?"

"Mmmm," said Ariel. "I think I'll call it a…BIGGERmajigger!"

Giggling, the two friends returned to the palace with Ariel's biggermajigger.

Ariel and Flounder were in Ariel's room playing with her biggermajigger when King Triton came in. Quickly, Ariel hid the human object under her tail.

"Ariel," said King Triton, "I've been thinking about what you said about our not spending enough time together, and I—er—I...Ariel, what are you hiding beneath your tail?"

"Nothing, Daddy..." said Ariel.

"A-RI-EL!" King Triton boomed. "Tell me what you are hiding!"

"It's a—biggermajigger," Ariel confessed, as she pulled the strange object out from under her tail.

"Another human thing? In my palace?" said King Triton. "Ariel, I've told you not to play with human things!"

Then, with a single swoop of his trident, King Triton destroyed the biggermajigger and left Ariel's room.

Close to tears, Ariel hurriedly swam away from the palace with Flounder.

"Oh! He makes me so angry," Ariel cried.

"Aw, don't be mad," said Flounder, trying to comfort his friend.

"Well, I AM!" said Ariel. "He wouldn't even let me explain."

"He just wants to make sure you're safe," explained Flounder.

"I am safe," said Ariel. "I'm so safe I never get to have any fun!"

Meanwhile, King Triton was in the royal barbershop getting his hair cut. The Sea King sighed. He had meant to tell Ariel that he wanted to spend more time with her, but instead he had ended up destroying her human biggermajigger in a fit of anger.

"Sebastian, those human things can lead to the ruin of the merpeople," said King Triton. "Why won't Ariel just leave them alone? Why is she so fascinated with these human things?"

"She's stubborn," answered Sebastian. "It runs in the family."

"I suppose it does," laughed the King. "I'd better apologize to her as soon as she gets home."

"Flounder, look!" cried Ariel. The two friends had swum to the edge of a deep abyss. A sparkling golden thing had caught Ariel's eye. "I'm going to swim down there to see what that is," Ariel said excitedly.

"Uh, Ariel?" said Flounder. "I'm not sure that's such a good idea. It looks kind of dark down there."

"Oh, Flounder, don't be such a guppy," Ariel said.

Ariel swam closer to the edge of the abyss and reached out for the shiny object. She saw that there were, in fact, two shiny objects, one large round one and another little golden one resting on a rock nearby. Although Ariel didn't know it, one of the objects was a charm bracelet, and the other was the key that unlocked the clasp to the bracelet. As Ariel reached for the bracelet, the key was swept deeper down into the dark abyss.

"This must be a human girl!" Ariel cried excitedly as she looked at a ballerina charm on the bracelet. "And this must be a human boy!" she said, pointing to a teddy bear charm. "He looks—well, he looks as if he has a nice—personality."

As she gazed at the pretty charm bracelet, Ariel began to wonder what humans did with this magical golden thing. She began testing it in different ways. She tried to put it in her hair, but it was too small. She tried to put it on her finger, but it was too big. She tried putting in her mouth, but it didn't taste very good. Finally she slipped it over her wrist.

"Look, Flounder!" she cried. "It fits!"

But as soon as she had spoken, Ariel realized that although the thing had easily slipped onto her wrist, she couldn't seem to slip it back off.

"Uh-oh," said Flounder.

Back at the palace, King Triton was practicing his apology with Sebastian.

"Ariel," King Triton recited, "I'm sorry I destroyed your biggerma—what?"

"Biggermajigger, Your Highness," said Sebastian.

"What a silly name," said Triton. "Can't I just say, 'Ariel, I'm sorry, but human things are dangerous, and as your father, I know what's best! Therefore, I forbid you...' "

Sebastian sighed.

"That wasn't a very good apology, was it, Sebastian?" asked King Triton.

"Well, Your Majesty, if I may be so bold," said Sebastian, "perhaps you should stop trying to recite your apology. A true apology comes from the heart and doesn't need to be rehearsed."

Ariel knew that she could not return to the palace and face her father with the shiny golden thing still stuck on her wrist.

Although Ariel and Flounder did not know the name or function of the key that belonged with the bracelet, Flounder had an idea. He thought maybe that little piece could help Ariel remove her bracelet.

"Hey, Ariel," he said excitedly. "Maybe that other little piece that got lost can help you!"

"Flounder, you're a genius!" cried Ariel. "All I have to do is swim down into the abyss to get it."

"No, Ariel! Wait!" Flounder pleaded. But it was too late.

Suddenly there was a loud sound of water swishing all around Ariel. Within moments she felt herself being twirled around and around in a giant whirlpool.

Flounder looked on in terror. "Ariel!" he cried. "What's happening?"

"It's a whirlpool!" cried Ariel. "Flounder, go get hel-l-l-p!"

Flounder watched helplessly as his friend got swept down into the deep abyss. "Ariel!" he cried.

Ariel kept spinning down and down when suddenly—WHAM! She landed on the top of a hard object and was thrown across the ocean floor.

"What was that?" she said out loud.

"Feeding time," replied a voice behind her.

"What?" said Ariel spinning around to face one of the strangest-looking creatures she had ever seen under the sea.

"My name's Barda," said the creature, "and that thing over there is the Flow Monster. Whenever he gets hungry, he creates a whirlpool and sucks in whatever gets in the way. Count yourself lucky. You must not be his favorite flavor. Otherwise you'd be somewhere inside his digestive tract right now."

"How do I get back home?" asked Ariel.

"You don't," Barda replied matter-of-factly. "We're all stuck. By the way, nice bracelet."

"Nice what?" asked Ariel.

"Bracelet. That thing around your wrist. I collect things like that. Keeps me busy," Barda said.

Suddenly Ariel found herself face-to-face with a creepy creature holding a bag.

"Psst," said the creepy creature. "What's the matter, dear? Lost and aloooooone? Come on over here and look inside my bag."

"Stay away from her," whispered Barda. "She'll eat anything— including you and me."

Soon Ariel found herself surrounded by all sorts of eerie creatures staring and grabbing at her. She felt as if she wanted to stay as close to Barda as possible.

"How am I ever going to get out of here?" she wondered quietly to herself.

"What's your rush?" asked one of the creatures.

"Stay with us," hissed another.

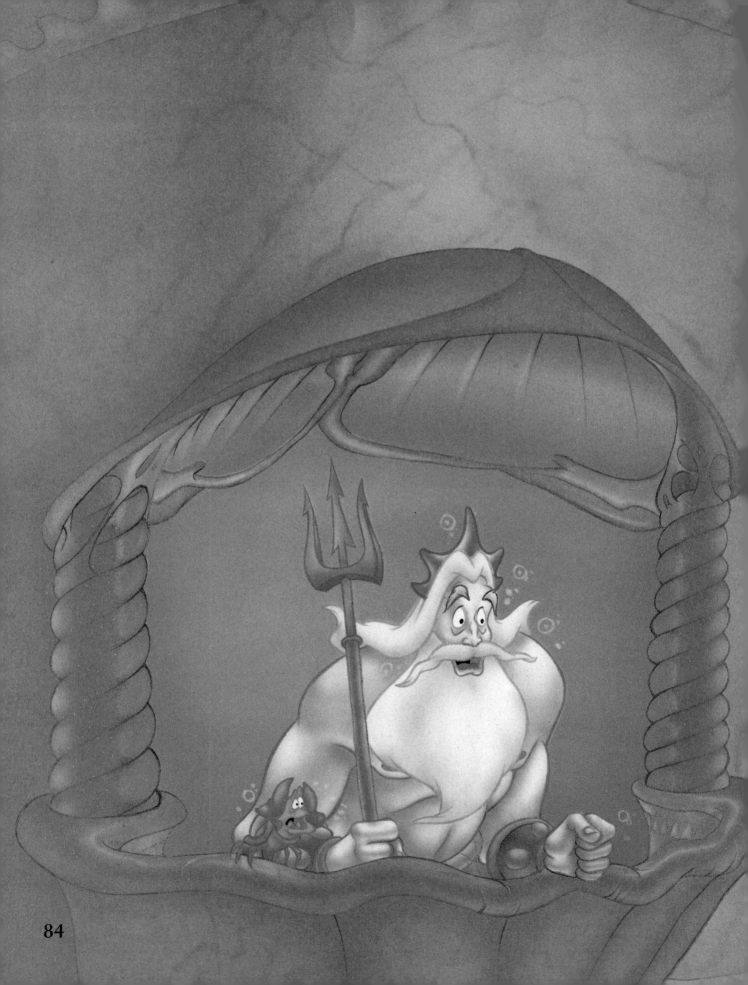

Meanwhile, high above Ariel, Flounder rushed as fast as his fins could carry him back to the palace. He swam right into King Triton's private quarters without even asking permission!

"Ariel!" Flounder panted to the King. "It's Ariel! We were swimming over a huge abyss when this big whirlpool sucked her down into the abyss and then…"

"Flounder!" Triton interrupted. "Take me there as fast as you can!"

And off they went, with Sebastian following close behind.

Soon Flounder led King Triton and Sebastian to the edge of the huge abyss that had swallowed the Little Mermaid.

"I'm going down there to get Ariel," said King Triton, as he swam into the abyss.

"Yaaah!" shouted Flounder who had gotten too close to the whirlpool and was being sucked in.

"What about meeeeeeee?" cried Sebastian. He was caught in the flow, too!

Soon all three were careening down, down, down in the whirlpool.

As they approached the bottom of the whirlpool, King Triton used all of his strength to aim his trident toward the invisible source of the powerful water flows. Finally he caught a glimpse of the sharpened teeth of the powerful Flow Monster. Aiming his trident carefully, King Triton managed to distract the hungry monster just enough to allow Flounder, Sebastian, and himself to slip past it.

Once they had safely moved beyond the Flow Monster, King Triton and his companions found themselves among the same lost souls that Ariel had encountered earlier.

"Ariel!" called King Triton desperately. He was afraid his Little Mermaid had been swallowed by the Flow Monster.

"Daddy?" cried a little voice. "Is that you?"

Just then, Ariel swam out of a small cavern with Barda close behind.

"Ariel!" cried King Triton, giving his daughter a big hug. "We were afraid you were—that we would never—"

"We're glad you're okay," said Flounder, smiling.

"We were worried," added Sebastian.

"Now let's go home," said King Triton.

"Uh—excuse me," interrupted Barda. "You're not going anywhere. Nobody can get out of this place. The Flow Monster only sucks creatures down into this gloomy place. He doesn't let them back out. We're all stuck here. Forever."

"This Flow Monster," asked King Triton, "is he feeding now?"

"No," said Barda, "but you have to be really strong and swim fast to be able to get by him before he begins his next whirlpool."

"I think I can do that," said King Triton. "Come on, Ariel. Flounder, Sebastian, hold onto my beard. We're getting out of here."

"What about Barda?" asked Ariel.

"Naw," said Barda. "I've gotten used to it down here. I think I'll stay."

"Thanks, Barda," said Ariel. "I won't forget you."

Then the powerful King Triton swam up with all his might and brought Ariel, Flounder, and Sebastian right up and out of the abyss.

"Hooray!" cried Flounder. "Let's go home!"

"No, wait!" said Ariel, swimming quickly away. "I have to do one last thing."

Ariel swam over to the ledge where the golden key still rested and picked up the small object. Then the Little Mermaid found a place on her wrist ornament where the key fit. She inserted the key and turned it. The bracelet magically slipped right off her wrist.

"It worked!" she cried. Then she grasped the bracelet and key in her hand and threw them toward the abyss. "Thank you, Barda," she whispered.

Just then, another whirlpool began.

"Ariel, get away from there," cried King Triton. "The Flow Monster is starting his whirlpool again."

He pulled his daughter close to him and swam her to safety.

As Ariel and King Triton swam back toward home together, they watched the golden human things get sucked into the abyss.

"Why did you put yourself in danger again like that?" King Triton asked angrily.

"Because I wanted to send the human ornament down to Barda to thank him for helping me," Ariel answered. "And besides, I don't need any more human ornaments. I'm happy with my mermaid ornaments."

King Triton smiled at his Little Mermaid. He knew she would soon be out looking for human treasures again. But for now she was safe, and that was all that mattered.

Back at the palace, Ariel turned to her father.

"You were great, Daddy," she said. "You saved us all."

"I don't feel great," the King replied.

"Why not?" asked Ariel.

"Ariel, I feel—" the King sighed. "I feel that I've let you down. From now on, I promise to listen more carefully—and spend more time with you."

"Thank you, Daddy," said Ariel as she gave her father a great big hug. "I'd really like that."

Stormy the Sea Horse

Ariel, the Little Mermaid, loved her freedom. Whenever she got a chance, she liked to go explore old shipwrecks or go up to the surface of the sea to look at the world above her.

One day she decided to ask her sisters to come along.

"Hey, you three!" Ariel called. "Do you want to go exploring?"

"No, thanks, Ariel," said Aquata. "We have things to do."

"Like our hair," giggled Andrina.

"And our nails," added Arista.

Ariel's sisters couldn't understand why she always wanted to see new things. There were already lots of nice things right inside the palace.

Ariel left her sisters and found her friend Flounder.

"Sure, I'll go exploring with you," said Flounder. "Let's try the royal stables. I heard they have a wild new sea horse. Wanna check it out?"

"Oh, yes!" said Ariel excitedly.

"He's beautiful," Ariel said as soon as she saw the sea horse. "What's his name?"

"We call him Stormy because he's a wild one," answered the royal sea horse trainer. "You be careful with him, Princess. We don't want ya gettin' hurt, now."

"He just wants to be free," said Ariel. "Don't you, Stormy?"
Stormy nuzzled Ariel's hand.
"That fella's not going free," said Ralph. "The King wants him tamed."

Ariel went directly to her father, King Triton, and asked him to let her learn to ride Stormy.

"Absolutely not!" roared King Triton. "That sea horse is too wild!"

That night Ariel tried again. "Daddy," she asked, "if Sebastian were to come with me, would you let me take sea horse riding lessons?"

"Sebastian!" the King said, laughing. "I don't think Sebastian would like that very much."

"But with Sebastian watching me," Ariel continued, "wouldn't you let me ride Stormy?"

"Stormy!" cried King Triton. "I already told you, Ariel. You are forbidden to go near that dangerous sea horse!"

"Oh, Flounder," Ariel said later in her room. "Daddy never lets me do anything."

"C'mon, Ariel," said Flounder. "There are plenty of fun things we can do without that giant sea horse."

"I'm not thinking about us, Flounder," Ariel said sadly. "I'm thinking about poor Stormy. I bet that if he could go exploring with us, he'd be much happier."

Meanwhile, King Triton was talking to Sebastian.

"What should I do with Ariel?" King Triton lamented. "Everything I do upsets her. I only want her to be safe."

"Your Majesty, if I may be so bold," said Sebastian, "perhaps you can let the girl visit with the sea horse without riding him…"

"Maybe you're right," the King said with a sigh. "But I'll depend on you to look after her."

"Hmmmm," thought Sebastian as soon as he left King Triton. "If I know that girl, she's sneaking over to the sea horse stables right now. I'd better hurry over there before she gets in trouble."

But as Sebastian scuttled toward the sea horse stables, he didn't pay attention to what he was stepping on.

"Hey!" cried a clam. "We're trying to sleep here! What's the big idea?"

The cranky clams were so angry that they shoved Sebastian right into Stormy's stall.

"Aaah!" cried Sebastian.

"Naaaaay!" cried Stormy.

But Ariel showed up and calmed Stormy down.

"Ariel," said Sebastian, "I don't think this is a good idea. Your father will be—"

But Ariel had already saddled the wild sea horse and was riding off.

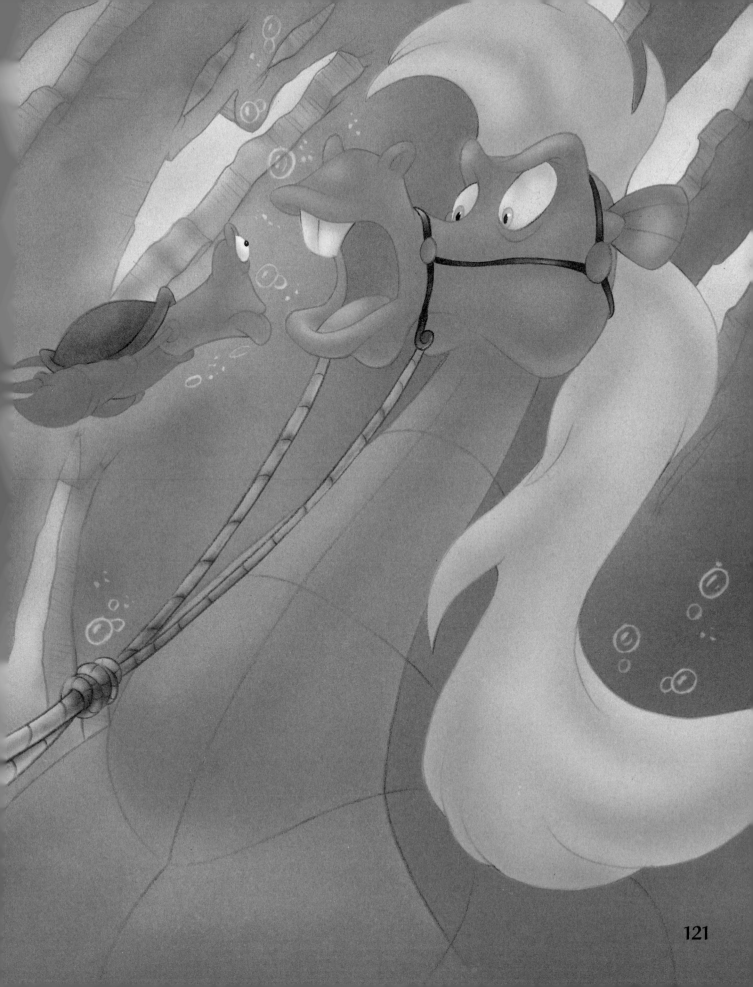

Sebastian raced after Ariel and Stormy, but he couldn't keep up with the powerful sea horse. Frantically, he looked out over the seascape to see if he could see the Little Mermaid.

"Something wrong, Sebastian?" came a deep voice behind him. Sebastian whirled around.

"Wrong?" Sebastian repeated. "Why, no, Your Majesty, no—oh, yes, there is. Ariel has ridden off on Stormy."

"Stormy!" cried the King. "Where's my royal sea horse? I must go after her!"

It didn't take King Triton very long to find Ariel and bring her back to the palace. After putting Stormy in the royal stables, the King turned to Ariel.

"You are never to go near that sea horse again!" cried King Triton. "Not even for visits. He's too dangerous."

"But Daddy…" said Ariel.

"That's final, Ariel," the King said.

But Ariel couldn't stop thinking about Stormy. She knew he was a good sea horse, but that he would never be happy in captivity. She knew that she needed to set him free. So that night she snuck into the royal stables once again.

Sebastian, who knew the Little Mermaid all too well, was watching the stables in case Ariel tried to sneak in to see Stormy again.

"C'mon, Stormy," Ariel whispered as she climbed on his back. But Stormy reared up and whinnied when he felt Ariel in his saddle.

"Ariel!" Sebastian cried. But she had already galloped away on the wild sea horse.

"Your Majesty!" Sebastian yelled as soon as he reached the royal palace. "Wake up! It's Ariel! She's run away with that sea horse, Stormy."

"I've already saddled up your sea horse for ya, King Triton," said the royal sea horse trainer, who had followed Sebastian. "If we start out right away, we may be able to catch them."

King Triton and Ralph galloped off while Sebastian and Flounder followed behind.

"Me? Ride a sea horse?" asked Sebastian. "Oh, no! I don't ride sea horses."

"S–s–stop talking and h–h–hang on," cried Flounder. "C'mon, Sebastian! We gotta save Ariel!"

Stormy had been so frightened when he and Ariel left the stables that he had gone straight to his wilderness home.

"Stormy, wait!" Ariel said. "I can't go there!"

Stormy whinnied wildly. He knew he was close to home, but he was still spooked.

"Stormy!" Ariel pleaded. "Please stop! I have to rest."

Ariel gently stroked Stormy's neck, and he finally slowed down enough to let her get off.

"Hey, boy," Ariel said soothingly to Stormy. "Let's just rest here for a while." Stormy nuzzled Ariel's hand and then settled down on the ocean floor. Ariel climbed up on a ledge and soon fell fast asleep.

Little did they know they were being watched—by two sea horse traders looking to capture a powerful sea horse!

As soon as Stormy saw the sea horse traders, he whinnied wildly and galloped off.

"After him!" yelled one of the traders.

Ariel woke up. "Stormy!" she cried as she frantically began swimming after Stormy and his pursuers.

139

Ariel swam as fast as she could, but she couldn't keep up with the horses. Soon she lost sight of them.

"Stormy, where are you?" she cried out.

Then Ariel heard a whinny off in the distance. Quickly she swam toward the sound.

Stormy was tied to a sea tree while the two sea horse traders sat nearby eating their supper.

"Shhh," Ariel said to Stormy. "I'll get us out of this."

Quickly the Little Mermaid untied Stormy and climbed up in his saddle. "C'mon, boy, let's go," she whispered.

Stormy galloped wildly away with Ariel on his back. He didn't even notice when he passed too closely under a sea vine.

Ariel hit her head and was knocked off Stormy's back!

"Ariel!" cried King Triton. He arrived just in time to catch the Little Mermaid as she fell toward the ocean floor. Stormy galloped off while King Triton carried Ariel home on his royal sea horse.

Back at the royal palace, Ariel recovered fully. Flounder and Sebastian were keeping her company when King Triton came in to visit her.

"Daddy, I'm sorry," Ariel said. "You were right. It was dangerous to ride Stormy."

"And you were right, too," King Triton replied. "Come with me. I want to show you something."

King Triton carried his daughter outside the palace. Just beyond the gates was Stormy.

"He must have come back to see if you were okay," King Triton said. "You were right, Ariel. He is a good sea horse. And because of that, I'm letting him go free—just as you wished."

Then, as Ariel and King Triton looked on, Stormy turned toward Ariel, gave one last whinny, and galloped happily off into the sea.

Sebastian's Medal of Honor

"Whoo-eee!" cried Flounder. "Perfect shot, Ariel!"

Flounder and Ariel were throwing seed pods at sea bubbles. Flounder grabbed a pod with his tail and flung it with all his might at a rising bubble. POP!

"Wow, Flounder!" said Ariel. "You're getting good at this!"

"Thanks, Ariel. Watch this one!" Flounder replied.

"Sebastian, look out!" cried Ariel.

Sebastian looked up just in time to see a seed pod heading straight at him. Sebastian ducked the seed pod, but popped right into a sea bubble instead!

Flounder and Ariel quickly swam to their friend and freed him.

"Sorry, Sebastian," said Flounder. "I didn't see you."

"That's all right," said Sebastian, "but I'm late for a meeting with the King. And you know how he is—he can't even find his own crown without me!"

Sebastian barely arrived in time for his morning meeting with King Triton.

"Hear ye, hear ye!" cried the royal herald. "First on the royal agenda: the weekly cleaning of the King's trident!"

"Oh, my!" thought Sebastian. "If I can polish that trident to perfection, King Triton will give me a medal and make me the royal trident polisher!"

Sebastian grasped the King's trident in his claw and began to rub. "Sebastian, NO!" cried King Triton. But it was too late. By rubbing the trident with seaweed, Sebastian had caused a bolt to shoot straight out of the King's powerful weapon.

The bolt bounced off the wall and nearly hit the royal herald.

"Uh—sorry, Your Majesty," whimpered Sebastian.

"That's all right, Sebastian," replied the king. "Now, let us proceed with the royal agenda."

"Uh, let's s-s-see," said the shaken herald. "Oh. Right. The issue of peace talks with the Sharkanians."

Sebastian's mind began to wander. If he, Sebastian, could only make peace with the Sharkanians, King Triton would finally give him the recognition he deserved. Maybe he would even get a medal.

"Your Majesty!" shouted Sebastian. "I have a great deal of experience with the Sharkanians. I once studied their language and culture. Perhaps if you were to send me as your ambassador…"

"Excellent, Sebastian!" said King Triton.

Quickly the King created an official document naming Sebastian as his official ambassador to Sharkania.

"Er—maybe I should get the dolphins to carry this for you," said King Triton when he saw Sebastian sinking under the weight of the document.

"Good idea, Your Majesty," Sebastian gasped.

Later that day, King Triton bid Sebastian good luck.

"Thank you, Sebastian," Triton said. "I must say I am impressed with your courage. Not many crustaceans would be brave enough to undertake such a dangerous mission."

"Danger? Hah! No problem, Your Majesty!" Sebastian said. "I'll be back in a couple of days with a peace agreement in my claw."

But as soon as he left the palace gates, Sebastian started to worry. "What am I doing?" he mumbled. "I am only a little crab. I don't know anything about Sharkanians, except that they eat crab and they have very sharp teeth."

Then Sebastian heard a voice behind him.

"Sebastian, wait up!" shouted Ariel. "Can we tag along?"

"Oh, well," Sebastian thought. "At least if I'm eaten, there will be witnesses, and I will be remembered as a hero."

"Whoa!" said Flounder as he looked at the entrance to the Sharkanians' headquarters. "That looks pretty spooky."

"I wonder why there are so many sunken ships around here," Ariel said.

"Maybe this wasn't such a good idea after all," said Sebastian. "Maybe we should come back later."

"Aw, c'mon," said Flounder. "You're an ambassador. They won't hurt you."

Soon the three friends swam through the gaping entryway to the Sharkanians' headquarters.

"Nobody's home," Sebastian said. "I guess we should leave now."

"Wait," said Ariel. "Let's ring the bell."

"I'll do it," Flounder announced happily as he began ringing the giant bell over Sebastian's head.

Suddenly, a door under Sebastian popped open, and a huge Sharkanian guard rose up out of it.

"Ah-hem," said Sebastian. "P-p-please excuse us. We must have come to the wrong place. We'll just be on our way now."

But Ariel spoke up bravely. "This is Ambassador Sebastian," she said, "and he is here to speak to Emperor Shaaga, if you please."

"Follow me," growled the guard.

As Sebastian, Ariel, and Flounder followed the guard down a long corridor, Sebastian's claws began to drag.

"C'mon, Sebastian," Flounder urged. "Stand up and act like a crab."

"It's okay, Sebastian," Ariel said as she gently pushed him forward. "The Emperor will love you."

Sebastian believed the Emperor would love him, all right— as dinner!

174

When Ariel and Flounder finally approached the Emperor, Sebastian was lagging far behind.

"Um, our ambassador has come in peace," Ariel said, stalling for time as she waited for Sebastian to catch up to them.

When Sebastian saw how brave the Little Mermaid was, he gathered up his courage to step forward.

"The Princess is right!" he cried. "We want peace."

"All right," growled Emperor Shaaga. "We accept."

"Oh," said Sebastian. "That wasn't so bad."

Emperor Shaaga insisted that Sebastian take back a gift for King Triton as a peace offering.

While they were waiting for the gift to be prepared, Ariel and Flounder decided to go exploring. But when they peeked through a hole in the wall of an old ship, they got a huge surprise: The Sharkanian guards were carefully hiding some Sharkanians in the chest they were preparing for King Triton.

"It's a trap," Ariel whispered as she listened to the Sharkanians' plan. "Those Sharkanians in the chest are going to open the gates to Daddy's palace and let the other Sharkanians in to attack. We have to go warn Daddy!"

But just as Flounder and Ariel turned to find Sebastian, two giant nets fell over them.

"Going somewhere?" snickered a Sharkanian guard.

Ariel and Flounder were put in chains.

The commander of the Sharkanian guards approached Ariel. "Write a note telling Sebastian to leave without you," he growled.

"I won't write any note," Ariel said.

"Write the note," said the commander, "or my lieutenant will fillet your little friend."

Ariel had no choice.

When Sebastian received Ariel's letter telling him to go home
alone, he figured that she and Flounder were exploring the area
with some newfound Sharkanian friends. He never suspected they
were in trouble.

So he left without them, carrying the Sharkanians' "gift" to
King Triton.

Meanwhile, Ariel had an idea, and whispered to Flounder. Flounder nodded quickly.

Then he said out loud, "Man, Ariel, these Sharkanians sure are a bunch of jellyfish. I could beat any one of them in a fin fight."

The Sharkanian guard smirked. "Oooo, I'm so scared," he said with a laugh.

"C'mon," said Ariel to the Sharkanian. "The rules are, you can only fight with your fins, so let me tie your hands first."

Minutes later, Ariel and Flounder were swimming away while the angry guard struggled to free himself.

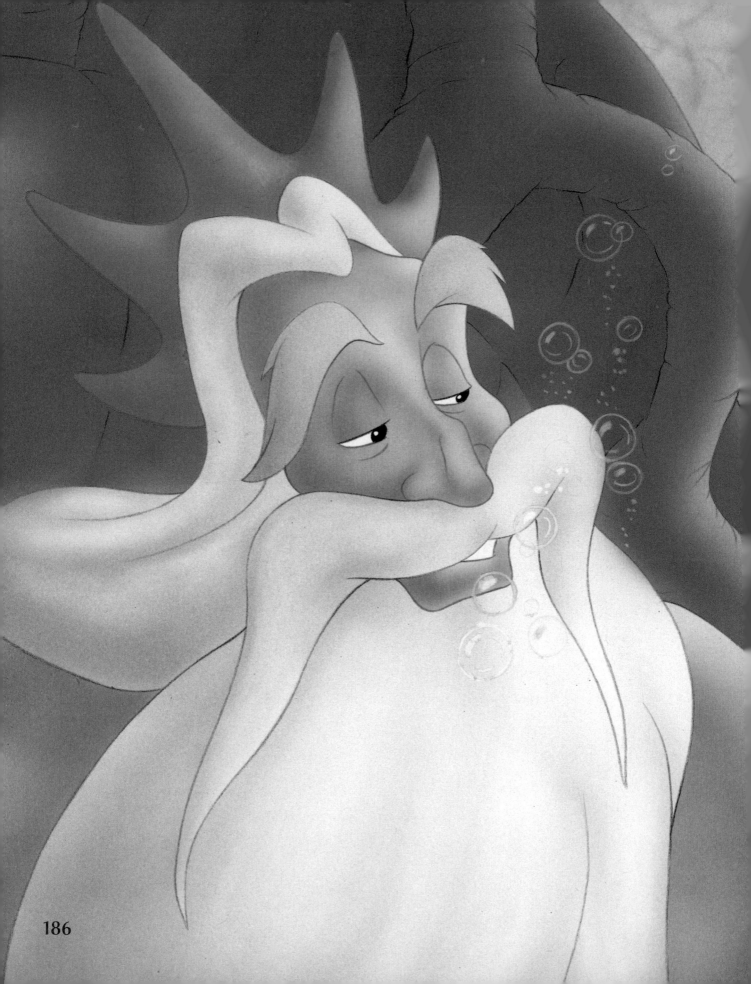

186

Back at King Triton's palace, Sebastian sat happily in the King's mighty hand.

"Ambassador Sebastian, you're a genius," King Triton said with a smile. "I'm very proud of your work making peace with the Sharkanians. In fact, I think you deserve your very own medal of honor."

"Oh, thank you, Your Majesty," said Sebastian.

But even as King Triton was congratulating Sebastian, his daughter had just barely slipped past the evil Sharkanian guards.

"We made it, Flounder!" Ariel cried. "Now we just need to get to my father in time to warn him of the Sharkanians' attack!"

King Triton's guards had carefully placed the Sharkanians' treasure chest in the King's treasure room. Soon the lid to the box popped open, and out slithered the Sharkanians.

"Look at all these treasures," said one. "I'll grab us a few souvenirs before we leave."

The two Sharkanians filled a bag with treasure and were sneaking out of the treasure room when Sebastian happened to pass by.

"Where are you going?" the crab demanded.

"That Sharkanian's not going anywhere!" cried Flounder. He took aim and flung a seed pod right at the Sharkanian's head. POW! The Sharkanian was knocked out cold as the bag of treasure fell on Sebastian.

Meanwhile, the other Sharkanian had gone to the palace gate and signaled to the Sharkanian attack force to enter.

But Ariel had awakened her father, warning him of the secret attack. As soon as the Sharkanians passed through the palace gates, the mighty sea king swam after them, zapping them with his powerful trident.

"Yeow!" cried the Sharkanians. They swam away as fast as they could.

"Your Majesty," Sebastian said the next morning, "please forgive me. I was tricked, you see—"

"Nonsense, Sebastian," said King Triton. "You did your best. And you helped me realize the true nature of those nasty creatures. In fact, I have a surprise for you—your very own medal of honor."

"Oh, thank you, Your Majesty," said Sebastian, looking eagerly at the giant medal. "But really, it's too much."

"I know," said the Sea King with a laugh. "I figured it might help keep you out of trouble."